Published by Modern Publishing
A Division of Unisystems, Inc.

Copyright © 1989 by Modern Publishing, a division of Unisystems, Inc.

TM – Pen Pals is a trademark of Modern Publishing,
a division of Unisystems, Inc.

® Honey Bear Books is a trademark owned by Honey Bear Productions, Inc.,
and is registered in the U.S. Patent and Trademark Office.

Printed in Belgium

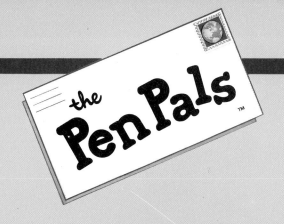

PETEY PRACTICES PEN-PAL-MANSHIP

Written and Illustrated by Susan Marino

MODERN PUBLISHING
A Division of Unisystems, Inc.
New York, New York 10022

"I'm sorry, Petey, but your arm is broken," the doctor said, as he put a cast on Petey's left arm. "You won't be able to use it for the next two months."

"Two months!" Petey cried.

"Don't worry, Petey," his mother said. "There'll still be plenty of time left to play ball by the time the cast comes off."

"But how will I be able to write letters to my pen pals?" Petey said. Last summer, at sleep-away camp, Petey had made friends with six other youngsters from all over the world, and they had formed a pen pal club.

"Why not learn to write with your right hand?" his father said.

Petey practiced and practiced, and soon his right hand penmanship was quite neat. He wrote letters to all his pen pals, and told them about his accident. "I wish you could all be here to sign my cast," he wrote.

"I wish I could sign it, too," Lucy Llama said aloud, when Petey's letter arrived at her home in Peru. "I *can* do the next best thing, though!" She sent a letter back to Petey right away, enclosing some colorful stickers of South American birds in the envelope. "These are to stick on your cast and remind you of me," Lucy wrote.

Lucy wrote to all the other pen pals and told them of her idea to decorate Petey's cast.

Greta Goat decorated Petey's get-well card with dried wild flowers that grew on the Alpine mountains where she lived, and sent along some matching flower stickers for his cast.

Chris Crocodile made some stickers of the African continent, and sent them to Petey along with a box of fresh Egyptian dates that grew on the trees in his backyard.

Billy Buck made pinecone and acorn stickers for Petey's cast. "Just like the ones that blanket the floor of my forest home in America," he wrote.

Kerry Kangaroo sent Petey stickers of the koala bears who lived near him in Australia.

Patsy Penguin made some stickers of the whales who swam by her house in Antarctica.

Soon, all the cards, letters and stickers were on their way to Petey in China.

Petey had become bored with staying at home. He'd read all his books, watched all the television he cared to, and was tired of his games and toys. He felt like he hadn't anything fun to do—

—until the mailman handed him six letters from his pen pals.

He read all the letters and get-well cards three times each, and stuck each sticker on his cast.

"This is the next best thing to having all my friends with me," he told his parents. "And I'm not going to be bored any longer—I have too many thank-you letters to write!"

THE WORLD OF

Pacific Ocean

PETEY PANDA

ASIA

KERRY KANGAROO

AUSTRALIA

PATSY PENGUIN

ANTARCTICA